Dragon's Leaf Collection

Adapted by Becky Matheson
Based on an original TV episode written by Steve Westren

SCHOLASTIC INC.
New York   Toronto   London   Auckland
Sydney   Mexico City   New Delhi   Hong Kong

ISBN 978-0-545-20058-5

Published by Scholastic Inc. SCHOLASTIC and associated logos
are trademarks and/or registered trademarks of Scholastic Inc.

12 11 10 9 8 7 6 5 4 3 2 1   11 12 13 14/0

Printed in the U.S.A. 40
First printing, July 2011

It was a nice fall day.
Dragon was in the park.

A leaf fell in front of him.

"Wow," Dragon said. "It's pretty!"

Dragon took the leaf home.

He wanted to find the perfect place
for his new leaf.

Dragon hung the leaf on his wall.
Then the leaf fell down.

Dragon put the leaf on his pillow.
Then his cat found the leaf!

Dragon tried to put the leaf in a vase.
The leaf did not fit.

Then Dragon put the leaf in his kitchen.
"Perfect!" he said.

"I want to collect more leaves," said Dragon.

Dragon's friends wanted to help!
Mailmouse brought Dragon one leaf.

Beaver brought Dragon many leaves.

"Hey, little blue dude," Alligator said.
"I brought you these cool leaves."

Ostrich brought some, too!

Dragon was happy to have nice friends.

But he was running out of places
for the leaves!

There were leaves in the bathtub.

There were leaves in his suitcase.

There were leaves everywhere.
Dragon could not even find his cat!

Dragon knew he had to do something.
But what?

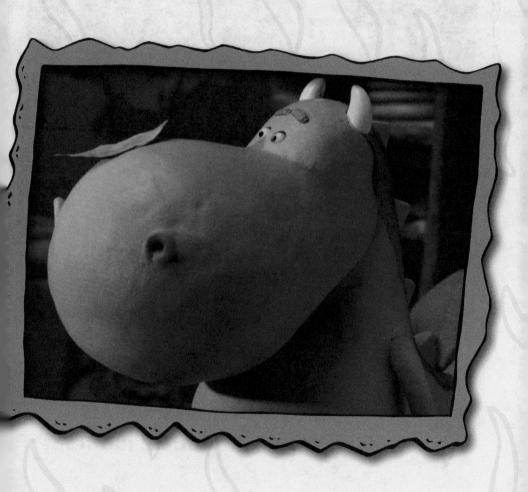

Dragon had a great idea.
He could write the trees a letter!

Dear Trees,
Please stop dropping
your leaves on the ground.
Love,
Dragon

Then Dragon brought his letter
to the trees.

Dragon saw something strange.

The trees had no leaves.

"I know!" said Dragon.

"I will tie my leaves to the trees."

Dragon found the perfect place
for his leaf collection.